This
Treasure Cove Story
belongs to

ZOOTROPOLIS

A CENTUM BOOK 978-1-912396-27-6
Published in Great Britain by Centum Books Ltd.
This edition published 2018.

3 5 7 9 10 8 6 4 2

Centum Books Ltd, 20 Devon Square, Newton Abbot,
Devon, TQ12 2HR, UK.

www.centumbooksltd.co.uk | books@centumbooksltd.co.uk
CENTUM BOOKS Limited Reg.No. 07641486.

A CIP catalogue record for this book is available
from the British Library.

Printed in China.

centum

Dısney
ZOOTROPOLIS

Adapted by
Heather Knowles

Illustrated by
Vivien Wu

Designed by
Alfred Giuliani

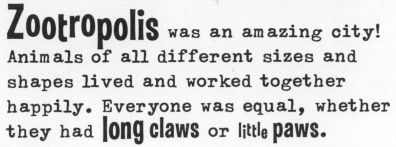

Zootropolis was an amazing city! Animals of all different sizes and shapes lived and worked together happily. Everyone was equal, whether they had **long claws** or little **paws.**

ANYONE CAN BE ANYTHING!

Even a small bunny from a farm in Bunnyburrow could achieve her dream job. **Judy Hopps** was the first bunny ever to join the Zootropolis Police Department!

Judy **hopped** with excitement as
she waited for her first assignment.

But when Police
Chief Bogo handed
her a machine for
issuing **parking
tickets,** her ears
fell. She wanted
to solve crimes,
not be a **meter maid.**

Still, Judy wanted to do a good job. Her **sharp hearing** alerted her to expired meters, and she wrote hundreds of parking tickets – before lunchtime!

At noon, Judy headed to a nearby
cafe for an **elephant-sized** treat. There
she met a little fox who was desperate
for a Jumbo-pop. His dad, **Nick,** was
out of cash, so Judy offered to pay.

But very soon, Judy
learned that Nick had
tricked her!

He melted the
Jumbo-pop...

...to create smaller **pawpsicles.**

Then he resold those for a **big** profit!

The next day, Judy got her chance.
Mrs Otterton's husband was missing,
and Judy offered to take the case.
Assistant Mayor Bellwether agreed, and
Mrs Otterton was so grateful! But Judy
had only **two days** to solve the crime!

Judy learned that Nick had seen Mr Otterton recently. She convinced the fox to help her by pulling her own trick: she used her **carrot pen** to record him talking about his shady business deals!

I NEVER PAY TAXES!

MYSTIC SPRING OASIS

Reluctantly, Nick helped Judy gather
clues all across **Zootropolis...** until they
reached the Rainforest District. The
plan was to question **Mr Manchas,** the last
animal to have seen the otter.

Nick and Judy found Mr Manchas,
but something was **wrong** with him.

He had gone **WILD!**

Nick and Judy worked together and escaped. They were becoming **friends**! Both of them wanted to solve this case and prove they could do important work.

Judy knew how to find their next lead! Using security-camera footage, she led Nick to a **scary building** on the edge of town.

Inside, they found more wild-eyed
animals — including the missing otter!
Why had these animals turned **Savage**?

A tip from an informer led Nick and Judy to an **abandoned subway station**. While **Nick** distracted the guards, **Judy** slipped into a subway car...

...that was also a **secret laboratory**! Judy saw a ram create a **serum** using a flower. She learned that the serum caused mammals

to turn **WILD**!

Nick and Judy grabbed the serum and ran... until they were cornered by **Assistant Mayor Bellwether!**

The sneaky sheep had created the serum because she knew that if animals with claws and fangs — **predators** — became savage, citizens would be scared of them. Then the smaller animals could lock them up and take over!

Bellwether shot a **dart** filled with the serum into Nick! The fox sank to all fours and started shaking. Bellwether **smiled.** She expected Nick to become savage and eat Judy!

But Nick **_didn't_** turn wild. He and
Judy had pulled their greatest trick.
They had **switched the serum** with
blueberry juice!

Nick and Judy gave the evidence
to **Chief Bogo,** and Bellwether was **arrested.**
All the animals who had gone savage –
including Mr Otterton – would soon be **cured.**

Judy and Nick had **solved the case,** and proved that they were far more than a dumb bunny and a sly fox. They were **partners** – and **best friends** – ready to fight crime in Zootropolis!

Treasure Cove Stories